THE PARTY CLUB

Rosie

Books by Anne Fine

Care of Henry

Nag Club

*How to Cross the Road
and Not Turn into a Pizza*

The Haunting of Pip Parker

The Jamie and Angus Stories

Jamie and Angus Together

Jamie and Angus Forever

Under a Silver Moon

The Only Child Club

THE PARTY CLUB

ANNE FINE

Illustrated by Arthur Robins

WALKER
BOOKS

First published 2015 by Walker Books Ltd
87 Vauxhall Walk, London SE11 5HJ

2 4 6 8 10 9 7 5 3 1

Text © 2015 Anne Fine
Illustrations © 2015 Arthur Robins

The right of Anne Fine and Arthur Robins to be identified as
author and illustrator respectively of this work has been asserted by
them in accordance with the Copyright, Designs and Patents Act 1988

This book has been typeset in Palatino

Printed and bound in Great Britain by Clays Ltd, St Ives plc

British Library Cataloguing in Publication Data:
a catalogue record for this book is available from the British Library

ISBN 978-1-4063-5312-9

www.walker.co.uk

For Zachary and Teddy
A.F.

With love to Harry, party boy
A.R.

~Chapter One~

Party Time!

Rosie rushed into the classroom on the first day of term to look at the brand-new Birthday List pinned on the wall.

There were nine names on it:

FARZANA   ELLIE

VICTORIA   OWEN

TOBY   MOLLY

GRACIE   ETHAN

SHERILYN

Farzana never had birthday parties, so that left eight. Victoria was next on the list. Her birthday was two weeks away.

Only two weeks! But Rosie hadn't had an invitation yet. Maybe they were in Victoria's bag right now, and before Miss Beaton came in to take the register, Victoria would fish them out and hand them round.

Then it would soon be party time!

Rosie loved birthday parties. Ever since she was tiny she'd adored everything about them: the bright balloons, the presents wrapped

10

in sparkly paper, the tubs of ice cream and the fancy cakes with candles on top, the party frocks, the special games – and goody bags at the end.

Parties! Oh, there was nothing better. Nothing was more fun.

Rosie couldn't wait. She hurried across the room to where Victoria was sitting.

Victoria looked up at the list. "But your name isn't there. Your birthday was last term. It's a long time till it comes round again."

"I didn't mean my birthday," Rosie explained. "I meant your party."

"But I'm not having one," Victoria told her.

Rosie was shocked. "Not *having* one?"

"Not this year," said Victoria. "This time, for my birthday treat, I'm going with my cousins to see the film *Sparkle and Daisy*. And afterwards we're going to Pizza Palace."

Rosie's face fell.

"So there's no party? No party at all?"

"No," said Victoria. "Sorry, Rosie, but there's no party at all."

Rosie tried to stay cheerful. "Oh, well. Toby's next on the list, and his birthday's only a few days after yours. So we'll have that one."

"No, we won't," said Victoria. "Because I got the idea from Toby in the first place. He's taking three friends bowling for his birthday."

Rosie looked over to see Toby pulling bright yellow envelopes decorated with balloons out of his school bag.

One... Two...

Rosie waited, biting her lip with excitement. Maybe Victoria had mixed things up and Toby was having a party as well as going bowling.

Three...

That was all. Toby closed his bag and handed the yellow envelopes to his best friends, Owen, Harry and Bradley.

Rosie moved closer to ask, "Are those your birthday invitations?"

Toby grinned. "Yes! We're going bowling!"

No party, then?

No, no party. I think that some of us might be getting a little too old for birthday parties.

Rosie's eyes widened in horror. Too old for birthday parties? What a *dreadful* thought.

~Chapter Two~

Disaster!

At breaktime, Rosie asked Gracie, "Will you be having a birthday party?"

"Of course," said Gracie. "I always do."

"Goody!" said Rosie. "I was worried that you might be the same as the others."

"What others?"

Rosie pointed. "Toby. And Victoria. They're doing something else instead."

"What?"

"Toby is going bowling with Owen, Harry and Bradley. And Victoria and her cousins are going to see *Sparkle and Daisy* and then out for pizza."

Really?

"Really?" Gracie stared over at Toby, then at Victoria. Rosie stood waiting for her to say something sensible, like: "They must be mad."

Or something cheering, like: "I'm sure they'll change their minds and have a party instead."

Or something cross-patch, like: "Well, isn't that *selfish*! What about the rest of us?"

But what she actually said was:

Gracie shook her head. "No, as well as Toby and Victoria. I'm going to ask Mum and Dad if I can take a friend to see *Sparkle and Daisy*, then go for pizza. I'll tell them that's what everyone in my class is doing now."

"Not everyone!" Rosie tried interrupting.

But Gracie wasn't listening. "And I think they'll be pleased. Mum's always saying that birthday parties are a lot of work. And Dad says that they leave him with a splitting headache and surely I'm getting too old for them now."

"No one is *ever* too—"

But Rosie couldn't finish. Gracie was squeezing the breath out of her with a giant hug. "Thanks so much for telling me, Rosie!

It's just in time. I wrote 'My Party Invitations' on the shopping list. And if you hadn't told me about Toby and Victoria, Dad would have bought them this evening and I would have filled them in and gone next door to give one to Shamaila. Then I would have had to go ahead and have the party."

Poor Rosie could have kicked herself for saying anything at all about Toby and Victoria's plans. After she'd watched

Gracie dance off, singing, "I'm going to see
Sparkle and Daisy! I'm going to see *Sparkle
and Daisy*!" she thought about the Birthday

List again.

The next name was

Sherilyn's.

No parties till

almost March, then.

What a disaster!

Were birthday

parties going out of fashion, like knitting?

Mrs Hall sometimes joked that if she hadn't

started Knitting Club, she'd be the only

person in the school who knew how to cast

on and off and do purl and ribbing stitch.

Would Rosie have to start a Party Club

to keep them going?

~Chapter Three~

"What would we miss the most?"

As soon as she was home from school, Rosie slid onto a chair at the kitchen table.

"Sit at the other end," her mother told her. "Your dad's about to start chopping green peppers."

"I don't mind," Rosie said.

"Maybe *you* don't," her dad said.

"But *I* do, because you usually steal so many bits that there aren't enough left."

"I promise I won't."

"All right. But I will be keeping an eye on you."

Rosie sat quietly, watching her father. *Slice, slice, slice. Chop, chop, chop.* She found it soothing.

After a moment, she took a deep breath and told her parents the terrible news. "Victoria and Toby and Gracie are giving up having birthday parties."

Rosie's dad broke off his chopping to look at her with real interest.

"Giving them up, eh? Is that right?"

"Yes."

He started chopping again. "Why's that, then?"

"Well," Rosie said uneasily, "Toby thinks some of us might be getting a bit too old for birthday parties with balloons and cupcakes and party poppers and ice cream and goody bags."

Her father, she noticed, was getting a rather faraway look in his eyes. "Does he indeed? Well, haven't I always said that I think Toby is a really bright and sensible boy!"

Rosie was getting suspicious.

Mind? If you gave up parties?

Are you saying that you wouldn't mind?

You wouldn't miss them?

"*Miss* them?" Her father grinned. "I wonder. Yes, I wonder. What would I miss the most? The arguments about how many children can fit in our house? Or all the fusses and sulks when we say you should invite someone you don't like much, but who invited you? Perhaps trailing round the shops looking for special party stuff you say we absolutely *must* have because it's your birthday? Would it be making sure the pushiest people don't win all the prizes? Or comforting the last guest when it turns out we're one goody bag short? Or maybe the clearing up afterwards?" He grinned at Rosie's mother. "Yes, it's so hard to decide what I would miss the most."

"That's not very nice," said Rosie.

"I can tell you what *I* wouldn't miss," said Rosie's mother. "Having to buy you a frilly party frock

every year in some brain-frying colour."

"I don't need a new frock *every* year," said Rosie. "And they're *supposed* to be in pretty colours."

"And I wouldn't miss having to calm your father down after he's spent hours making perfect iced cupcakes, only to find that your baby brother has stuck his thumb into the top of every single one."

"That only happened once," said Rosie. "And it was your fault because you told

Daddy that Charlie was safely in the other room watching *Teletubbies*."

Her mother made a face. "All right. Forget that one. But I definitely wouldn't miss watching the other parents take off in a shower of sparks to enjoy three wonderful hours of peace and quiet."

"You'd do that too," Rosie accused her, "if we didn't have Charlie. You know you would. So that one isn't fair."

Her father was grinning again. "Well, I can tell you that neither your mother nor I would miss watching you and your friends eat so many sugary foods that you start jumping around like hens on a hot roof."

"We're playing *party* games! That's what you *do*."

"Maybe it is," said her father. "And maybe that's why we think going to see a film and eating at Pizza Palace is quite a good idea."

Rosie was furious with both of them. Scooping up a handful of chopped green pepper, she slid off her chair and made for the door.

"Hey!" called her father. "Bring those back!"

But he was too late. Rosie had already stuffed them in her mouth.

~Chapter Four~

Good Things
About Birthday Parties

Up in her bedroom, Rosie made a list. She tore a sheet of paper from the pink perfumed pad that Sherilyn had given her at her last party. Across the top she wrote:

My List of Good Things
About Birthday Parties

She sat and thought. Finally, she wrote:

1. They're friendly because you can invite lots of people. and even if you don't have much money you can bake cakes for almost nothing, and you don't have to have a goody bag for everyone at the end.

Rosie thought some more.

2. You use more imagination at a party. Seeing a film is just like watching a big telly. But when I won Owen's make-something-with-ice-lolly-sticks party competition, everyone thought my peacock's tail was brilliant.

Rosie chewed the end of her pencil. Then

she wrote:

3. Pin-the-tail-on-the-donkey
games are good for your
see-in-the-dark-skills, which
are useful if the lights in your
house go out without warning.

Rosie read her list through, then took it

down to the kitchen. "This is my list of good

things about birthday parties," she told her

parents. "And after you read it, you'll have

to agree that seeing a film and going for a

pizza are not at all

the best things

to do."

She slammed the list down on the table. Then, thinking it would be best to give her parents time to see how wrong they were, she wandered off to see what Charlie was doing.

Her brother was watching a cartoon. It was a good one, so Rosie slumped beside him on the sofa and stayed there until it was finished.

~Chapter Five~

Bad Things
About Birthday Parties

As soon as the cartoon was over, Rosie went

back into the kitchen to ask her parents,

"Have you read my list?"

"We certainly have," her mother told her.

"Not only that, but we've made a list of our

own."

She pushed a sheet of paper across the

table to Rosie. The heading said:

Our List of Bad Things About Birthday Parties

Just like Rosie's own list, this one had three things. The first said:

1. Parties can be a bit of a worry.

"Parties don't worry people," Rosie argued.

"Sometimes they do," said her father. "What about that party when Molly put a pebble in her ear and couldn't get it out again?"

"But that was years ago!" said Rosie. "Molly and I were in *nursery*."

"And the time Ethan ate two whole tablespoonfuls of sand?"

"That was a *dare*."

"If parties aren't a bit of a worry," said Rosie's mother, "why are we always having to come outside to tell Victoria not to work Charlie's swing up so high it might go over the top?"

"She's only showing off," said Rosie. "Victoria knows when to stop."

To change the subject, she looked at the next thing on the list.

2. Parties are messy.

"Parties aren't messy," said Rosie.

"Yes, they are," said her father. "If parties aren't messy, why do I keep finding toy plastic sharks and bits of Mr Potato Head in the vegetable rack weeks after they finish? If parties aren't messy, why is your mother still coming across mouldy lumps of birthday cake down the back of the sofa from your last one? If parties aren't messy—"

"All right!" Rosie interrupted. "Some parties can be a little messy, I admit. What's your third thing?"

She looked down at her parents' list.
It said:

3. You need so much STUFF.

"What stuff?" demanded Rosie.

"Oh, you know." Rosie's
mother spread her hands.
"Party invitations. Party plates."

"Party napkins," Rosie's
dad reminded her. "And
party hats."

"And party drinks and
straws and party sausages
and cheese straws."

"I'm running out of fingers."

"Party poppers and those party blow-out things that make a horrid squawk."

"Don't forget party balloons."

"Stop it!" said Rosie. "Both of you, stop it!"

"Party-cake candles," her father went on as if she hadn't said a word. "And party-game prizes, of course."

Rosie clapped her hands over her ears.

"Not listening!" she shouted. "I'm not listening any more!"

But she could still hear what her parents said.

"Not to mention the goody bags."

"Filled with all those sweets and party favours."

With her hands still clamped over her ears, Rosie stomped out of the room.

~Chapter Six~

Party Club

"That's it, then!" Rosie muttered to herself. "I'll get no help from Mum and Dad. It's up to me. I'm just like Mrs Hall, who had to start a club to stop the whole school from not knowing how to knit. I'm going to have to start a club to save my class from having no birthday parties."

Mrs Hall had come into all the classrooms,

one by one, to ask how many people wanted to learn to knit. "No point in starting a club if I'm the only one in it!" she'd joked.

Rosie had better do the same.

She tore another sheet of paper off her pad and wrote across the top in giant fancy letters:

✰ PARTY CLUB ✰

She thought for a moment, then added:

1. Rosie Marshall

She left a space for all the other names. Rosie wouldn't dare go round the whole school, but she was sure she could get most of the people in her class keen on the idea of having parties again.

Mrs Hall had been cunning. She'd carried round a lovely long scarf in rainbow stripes. "Join my club," she had tempted them, "and you'll be able to knit something like this."

A forest of hands had shot up. Everyone was suddenly excited about the idea of a knitting club.

Well, Rosie could be cunning too. She'd think of wonderful ideas for parties and tempt them all into putting their names on her list.

Early next morning, Rosie looked around the classroom. Who should she speak to first?

Not Owen, because he'd probably decide to do the same as Toby. They were best friends. Not Sherilyn, either. Gracie hadn't said who she was inviting to the film, but she'd probably choose Sherilyn because they

lived on the same street and often did things together. So Sherilyn would probably copy Gracie and not have a party.

But that still left Ellie, Ethan and Molly. And that was only this term's birthdays.

How about Ellie? She was sitting by herself, sharpening her pencil before lessons began.

Yes, Ellie! Ellie had always loved parties. She was the perfect person for Rosie to go to first with her brilliant idea.

~Chapter Seven~

Ghost Party

Rosie walked over to Ellie. "Ellie, do you like the idea of a ghost party?"

Ellie looked up. "A ghost party? Oh, ace! I adore ghouls and witches and spooks!" She called to Molly and Ethan. "Rosie is having a ghost party! Isn't that a great idea?"

Before Rosie could explain, Ethan had rushed over. "A ghost party? Yes! Dylan near me had one at Halloween. His mum stuck black bat shapes over the windows to make the rooms scary dark. She hung strands of wool from the ceiling and every time they brushed your face it creeped you out, even though you were expecting it!"

Rosie tried to explain. "I'm not really—"

But no one was listening. They'd all gathered round Ethan, who was telling them more about Dylan's party. "Then everyone put on blindfolds to go in the Spooks Museum they'd made in their garage."

"I heard about that!" said Molly. "Dylan's brother made you stick your finger in what he said was blood, though it was really only olive oil."

"Then you had to feel the dead pirates' eyeballs," said Ethan. "They were just peeled grapes but Dylan said they felt *disgusting*."

"Then you had to squeeze the vampire's guts."

"And that was only cooked spaghetti."

"It must have been a brilliant party," said Victoria wistfully.

"I wish I'd been invited!" agreed Farzana.

Rosie pulled out her Party Club list and held her pen ready. They all sounded excited. Ethan's description of the party had been a lot more appealing than  Mrs Hall's rainbow scarf. Probably everyone would want to join her club now.

Then Terri-Ann, who had been listening, said, "But don't forget the terrible trouble afterwards."

Everyone turned to ask, "What terrible trouble?"

"Didn't you hear?" said Terri-Ann. "While she was waiting for her turn to go in the Spooks Museum, Lily told a story about a ghost who jumped out of a cracked mirror to kidnap a little girl and turn her into a ghost as well. And after that, in this story, every time the girl's brother looked in the mirror, he didn't see his own eyes staring back at him. He saw his sister's eyes, because she was trapped behind the mirror."

"What's wrong with *that*?" demanded Ethan. "It sounds like a good, scary story."

"Maybe it is," said Terri-Ann. "But someone who heard it told the story to Holly Worth later."

They all knew Holly Worth. Holly Worth was scared of everything – even dogs barking and the most pathetic fireworks.

"After that," Terri-Ann said, "Holly was so scared of mirrors that she wouldn't go to any lavatory by herself. Even at home, she had to have her mother in the doorway to feel safe. So Mrs Worth went round to Dylan's house to complain."

They all knew
Mrs Worth.
She waited for
Holly at the
gates, telling
people off for
dropping litter
or for shouting
too loudly.

Or even for just mucking about on their
way out of school.

"I wouldn't want Mrs Worth to come to
my house after a party to complain,"
admitted Ethan.

"Neither would I." Victoria shivered.

"No. Better stay away from ghost parties..."

Sighing, Rosie folded her list and put it in her bag. She'd have to try to tempt them with some other sort of party tomorrow.

~Chapter Eight~

Clown Parties and Monster Parties

Next morning, on the walk to school, Rosie slid her hand into her pocket to check that her Party Club list was safe. Hers was still the only name on it, but all she needed was good ideas to make more people join.

What about a clown party? Would her class be keen on that idea?

Well, even if they would, she didn't care! She wasn't going to suggest it. Rosie *hated* clowns. She didn't tell her friends in case they thought she was as babyish as Holly Worth. But Rosie thought clowns were the creepiest things in the whole world. She didn't even think that they were funny, with their enormous shoes and tiny cars that kept having explosions and breaking down.

She hated everything about them. Their silly too-big clothes. Their huge mitteny hands. She hated their messy orange hair and chalk-white faces with the painted smiles or tears. Mostly, she hated that you couldn't tell what they were thinking. The clowns with happy faces might really be sad inside – practically *weeping*. The ones with tragic faces might be feeling perfectly cheery.

Clowns worried Rosie horribly.

No. No clown parties. No!

How about a monster party? Monsters were almost as much fun as ghosts – and much, much better than clowns. Yes. That's what she'd tempt them with today. The idea would remind them how much fun parties could be. They'd all queue up to put their names on her list.

Rosie walked so slowly, daydreaming about her club, that she was the last one through the gates. Assembly was starting, so there was no time for her to talk to anyone till they were back in the classroom. Then, while Miss Beaton was admiring the new plaster cast on Tamsin's foot, Rosie said loudly:

Rosie was startled. Before she could even ask what wasn't nice about it, Ethan pitched in. "No. That's not even funny."

"I think it's almost *spiteful*," Leila said.

Rosie looked around. They were all staring at her as if she had said something horribly mean.

What are you on about?

She carried on, "All I said was, 'Who thinks a monster party would be really good fun?' What's wrong with *that*?"

Victoria put a protective arm round Rosie. "See? Rosie isn't trying to be nasty. She just doesn't know."

"Know *what*?" demanded Rosie.

Victoria pointed to Tamsin, who was hobbling towards them in her new plaster cast.

"You came too late to hear!" Tamsin said excitedly to Rosie. "I broke my foot! On Saturday, I went to my cousin's party and he made me wear a mask with tiny eyeholes."

"Why?" Rosie asked her.

"Because it was a stupid monster party!"
Tamsin said. "One of my cousins was
Godzilla and the other was King Kong.
My sister had to be Bigfoot, and my brother
was Frankenstein's monster. By the time
I got to pick, the only costume left was the

Loch Ness monster, and it had such small
eyeholes that I couldn't see. I tripped on the
porch step and broke my foot."

Rosie was sorry for Tamsin – and for
herself as well. She'd had such high hopes!
But clearly this was not the day to talk about
monster parties.

Getting everyone excited about parties
again would just have to wait.

~Chapter Nine~

"Pick up that litter, please, Rosie."

At breaktime, Rosie pulled the list of Party Club members out of her pocket. She really wanted to pin it on the wall beside the Birthday List, but it looked very short with only her own name.

So Rosie added Charlie's. Her little brother hadn't had a party yet, and Mum and Dad had said they wouldn't bother till he was old enough to start complaining. But it made the list look better. Now there were two names.

Rosie looked up. Sherilyn and Gracie were sitting together in the corner, talking. Rosie scowled. She was quite sure that Gracie must have gone home and asked her parents if she could change her birthday plans, and invite Sherilyn to come with her to see *Sparkle and Daisy*, then go for a pizza, instead of having a party.

But there was still Ellie and Ethan and
Molly. They might join her club.

Ethan was nearest, so Rosie walked
across to ask:

Ethan, do you want to join my Party Club?

What's a Party Club?

Rosie explained, "We promise one
another that when it's our birthday, we'll
do the same as usual and have a party.

We won't just go off and do something else."

"Sorry," said Ethan. "My mum's said I can take a friend to the new trampoline centre. So I'll be doing that."

Rosie sighed and carried the list over to where Ellie and Molly were leaning on the windowsill, watching the rain fall in spots on the puddles.

"Will you be having parties?" Rosie asked.

"Your names are on the Birthday List, and
I'm starting a club."

"What sort of club?" asked Ellie.

"Like Knitting Club," said Rosie, "except
that instead of learning knitting, we'll be
having birthday parties."

"What, every Wednesday lunchtime?"

"Of course not," Rosie said. "Just when
our birthday comes round."

"I'm not sure what I'm doing for my
birthday yet," said Ellie. "I might have a
party. And I might not.
I can't decide."

"I'm not sure either,"
said Molly, "because my

birthday's in the very last week of term and we're going off on holiday straight after. Mum says that, if I want, I can skip having a party and go to the water park near where we're staying on two extra days."

"*Two* extra days?" said Ellie. "That's pretty good because my mum says water parks are really expensive."

"Yes," agreed Molly. "But my mum says that birthday parties cost the earth. And I think I might be getting a bit bored with them anyway."

Rosie gave up. She looked down at the sheet of paper on which she'd written Party Club in such hopeful, fancy letters.

Then, sighing, she tore it into little pieces and watched them sadly as they floated to the floor.

Miss Beaton called across the room. "Pick up that litter, please, Rosie! And, everyone else, go back and sit in your places. Breaktime is over now. Take out your workbooks."

Another lesson had begun.

~Chapter Ten~

"Me? Do you mean me?"

Miss Beaton kept them busy until lunchtime. That didn't bother Rosie. She quite liked working hard, and anyway, she wasn't in the mood for whispering and passing notes.

She was fed up with everyone.

She was fed up with Miss Beaton for snapping at her about the bits of paper she'd dropped. She was fed up with some of the

people on the Birthday List for making the wrong plans and others for not making plans at all. She was fed up with her mum and dad for being so rude about parties. She was even fed up with Charlie for not being old enough to complain about not having a party himself.

And it was about a *hundred years* till the next birthday of her own.

Rosie was just fed up.

At lunchtime, it was still raining. "You'll have to stay inside till it's our turn to go to the dining hall," Miss Beaton said. "It's far too wet for outside play."

Rosie just shrugged and pulled her book out of her cubbyhole. She settled down to read. Out of the corner of her eye, she did see Gracie picking her way towards her between the desks, but Rosie wasn't in the mood to talk to anyone.

She kept her head down.

"Rosie?"

Gracie was tapping her on the shoulder. Rosie pretended she hadn't noticed,

but Gracie kept tapping and said her name

louder. "Rosie!"

Rosie looked up.

I have an important question. Are you free on my birthday weekend? Can you come with me to see *Sparkle and Daisy?*

Me? Do you mean *me?*

"Of course," said Gracie. "Sherilyn's coming too. Mum says I can bring two friends. And she says we can go out to eat after, but she doesn't want to go to Pizza Palace. She told me to ask if you like Chinese food because, if you do, we could go to Loon Fung instead."

"I *adore* Chinese food!" said Rosie. "I love it more than anything in the whole wide world!"

"So will you come?"

"I'll come!"

Rosie closed her book and she and

Gracie went back across the room to talk

to Sherilyn. They talked about the Chinese

food that they liked best, and what good

fun it was to swivel the Lazy Susan tray

in the middle of the table so that what you

liked eating most spun round in front of

you again.

"You will remember?" Gracie asked

anxiously. "Because Mum says that as it's

only you two, there's no need for proper invitations. But you won't *forget*?"

Sherilyn looked at Rosie and Rosie looked back at Sherilyn. Both of them grinned.

No, I absolutely promise you we won't forget.

And you don't want to bother with special invitations anyway. Sometimes I think that some of us are getting a little too old for some of that fancy birthday party stuff.

Rosie heard an echo in her head, and blushed.

And then she grinned again. After all, there would be plenty of parties in the future. All sorts of parties, and they'd all be fun. But right now she was going to see *Sparkle and Daisy*! And after that, eat Chinese food with her friends.

Oh, wonderful! Who needed the Party Club?

Not Rosie. No, not any more.

Anne Fine is a distinguished writer for adults and children. She has won many awards for her children's books, including the Carnegie Medal twice, the Whitbread Children's Book of the Year Award twice, the Smarties Book Prize and the Guardian Children's Fiction Prize. In 2001, Anne became Children's Laureate and in 2003, she was awarded an OBE. Anne has two grown-up daughters and lives in County Durham.

Arthur Robins has illustrated numerous children's books and exhibited his work in London. He has won a Gold Award in the Nestlé Smarties Book Prize and a Design & Art Direction Silver Award. In 2001, he illustrated the Royal Mail Christmas stamps. Arthur lives in Surrey.

You can find out more about Anne Fine and Arthur Robins by visiting their websites at **www.annefine.co.uk** and **www.artrobins.com**